I0538652

The Launderer

Don Allen

This book is a work of fiction, including, but not limited to, the accuracy of events, people, and places depicted, and opinions expressed. Names, characters, places, and incidents are the product of the author's imagination or are used fictitiously. Any resemblance to actual events, locations, or persons, living or dead, is coincidental.

All rights reserved.
Copyright © 2023 by Don Allen

No part of this book may be reproduced in any written, electronic, recording, or photocopying without written permission from the author.

Cover, Don Allen, *Cash* - digital art

ISBN: 979-8-9877821-9-4
eISBN: 979-8-9877821-8-7

Publisher: Don Allen

Also by Don Allen

Sean Murphy Series
Satisfaction
Chaos

Other Stories
Dog Walker
Check for Junk

Dedication:

To my late wife Barbara
who would have enjoyed Sean Murphy
and his adventures.

1 The Call

It's been quiet at Eyeball for the past few weeks. By quiet, I mean no international mayhem, drug cartels, terrorists, or dead bodies on the doorstep. I'm Sean Murphy. Since working at Eyeball Inc., I've been chased by North Korean thugs, battled cartel drug lords, frustrated a terrorist ring, and been on the FBI's most wanted list. I'm a former Army Ranger, enlisted. Over the years I participated in several black ops, some of which Navy SEALs shied away from most in the Middle East, a few in Africa, and most recently in Afghanistan. Colonel Anderson is my former commanding officer, we are both retired, and Eyeball is the Colonel's hobby. Eyeball is a security firm located just outside Richmond, Virginia, specializing in providing unique services to this nation's 'alphabet' agencies. Our bread 'n butter work that keeps the lights on and provides a good cover is mundane rent-a-cop contracts. But as the need arises, Anderson has assembled a small group that handles discrete, off-the-book projects for our clients.

As I said, it is quiet. I am one of Anderson's senior operatives, and I am bored stiff running specialized training classes that we've been contracted to provide. I need a distraction.

Late one afternoon, I got a phone call from Jeffrey. Jeffrey is my son-in-law, Wanda's husband. He is a high-priced financial guru working in New York City. From what Wanda has said and looking at their lifestyle, he is doing okay.

He sounds a bit panicked. "Sean, I think I need your help. Can I meet with you tomorrow?"

Now Jeffery and I have never had that much of a connection. From the tone of his voice, a twinge of concern crosses my gut, concern for Wanda and the twins, Arnold and Millie, who are now ten years old.

"Sure; where and how would you like to meet," I respond.

"I'll take the commuter shuttle to DC; we can meet in one of United's Premier Member meeting rooms at National Airport. I'll be there at 10:35 in the morning." And he adds, "Try to look non-descript; I may be followed. I'll explain. Please don't tell anyone of this meeting."

My curiosity is peaked. This is not the Jeffrey I know.

Early Tuesday morning I find myself in I-95 rush hour traffic. Traffic has not improved since our last meeting with the Director of the Department of Transportation last fall. Anticipating traffic, I left early and arrived at National Airport at 9:45. At ten, I went into the airport lounge looking for the United's Premier Member meeting rooms. They are on the other side of the TSA screening area and are only accessible to travelers. I have to buy a ticket. Going to the United counter, I pay cash for a ticket on the noon shuttle to New

York. I get a couple of sideway stares as I traverse the TSA checkpoint; I have no luggage. Access to the United's Premier Club area is not a problem. Eyeball is a member, and the young lady at the door smiles as I flash my card.

I'm just finishing my coffee when Jeffery arrives. He does not look at me as he goes to the concierge desk. The clerk gives him a magnetic pass card. Looking at me, he walks to the door labeled '3,' swipes the card, and waits for me. It's a small conference room with a table and eight chairs.

"Dad, thanks for coming. I'm scared shitless and don't know what to do," he blurts out.

"Okay, start at the beginning. It can't be all that bad."

Jeffery takes a deep breath and starts. "In early April, I was given a fully 'comped' weekend for two at the Foxwoods Resort Casino. This was given to me by one of my new clients. He was very pleased after I helped him move considerable assets to more secure locations."

"Secure locations?" I ask.

Looking somewhat embarrassed, he says, "To the Caribbean."

"Okay, go on," I say.

"As I said, he was happy with my services and gave me a voucher for Foxwoods. Wanda and I decided to take a short break from the twins. We used the voucher on the last weekend of April, two months ago. I took my laptop with me to track a few ongoing projects without giving it a second thought. I kept it in the room's safe when we went to the casino or out to eat. Our IT people assured me it was inaccessible without scanning my thumbprint, and all data was fully encrypted.

3

"This past Friday I got a call telling me they, and I don't know who they are, were going to take over my accounts. No one would know who they were. If I reported this, they would take Wanda and the kids. To demonstrate what they could do, I was directed to one of my more sensitive accounts and told to look for recent wire transfers. I found the transfers, two transfers actually. They were to the twins' college accounts."

"I take it you have not contacted the police, and the account pilfered belongs to not-so-nice people. I'm at a loss here as to what I can do. Can I call Dillion?"

"Who is Dillion?"

"Dillion is with the FBI. I've worked with him several times in the past. He is discrete."

"I'd rather you didn't," Jeffery says.

"It's your call, but if I read this right, you are being set up to look like you are skimming money from an account owned by who, the mob? This is not good; you need help. Dillion may be able to provide it."

Jeffery finally agrees. I call Dillion's office, and unexpectedly he's in. I tell him I need some help and can he meet me at National Airport. Reluctantly he agrees and says he'll be there in an hour.

Forty minutes later he slips into the meeting room. Jeffery retells his story, and Dillion asks a few questions. Dillion asks Jeffery if there is any video of his new client. Jeffery thinks there is. Dillion asks him to get a copy and send it to me discreetly.

2 Buy In

Later that week Jeffrey calls. "I just texted you pictures taken from our security videos. I couldn't get copies of the videos without raising questions, but I got some still clips claiming I needed them for my client files. There are three pictures, all providing good detail."

I open the texts, and the pictures are good. If this guy is in the FBI database, he'll be identified. "Jeffery, sit tight and don't do anything. I'll get back to you in a day or two."

I call Dillion and tell him what I have. He suggests a face-to-face handoff. I print three sets of 8X10 prints and head up the road to Quantico. Dillion meets me at the FBI forensic lab.

We get some coffee and claim one of the smaller conference rooms. "These are good," Dillon says. He calls in Marty, one of the crime techs. "Marty, here are some photos; see if you can get a hit on them in our database. The only name I have to go with them is Walter Williams, but that is probably an alias." Marty leaves, promising to be back shortly.

"Sean," Dillion starts, "I think Jeffrey is being set. I'm guessing some of his clients operate just this side of not wanting to draw our attention. I'm also guessing our Mr. Williams is taking advantage of this. It's likely that Jeffrey will be the odd man out when the shit hits the fan. He knows he has a problem, but I think the problem far exceeds his fears."

Close to an hour later, there is a knock on the door, and Marty is back. "Mr. Dillion, our Walter Williams's real name is Sydney Trocheck. He's been linked with several shakedowns and is allegedly a money launderer. Clients are reported to include drug cartels, third world dictators, and of course, the expected run-of-the-mill mobsters."

"Thanks," Dillon says. "Sit while I run his name through some secure databases."

As Dillion's fingers manipulate his keyboard Marty and I talk.

"From what I found in our database Trocheck appears to be an elusive figure. He, under several aliases, has been linked to several crimes, but there is never enough to charge him. Trocheck is just one of those background figures that we know is guilty but not indictable."

After a few minutes, Dillion becomes tired of caressing his keyboard and is back with us. "Marty's right. Trocheck is one of those phantom figures we want but can't get. This restricted database suggests Trocheck operates out of Idaho, where he has close ties with several Indian casinos."

We mull this around for a few minutes, and Dillion asks, "Do you think we can get Jeffrey to help bring Trocheck down?"

"In these types of crimes, do the victims' families get sucked in?" I ask.

"In a high number of cases, families eventually suffer financially, and in a moderate number of cases, families suffer assaults or kidnappings."

"So," I say, "Wanda and the twins are at risk here. I'll see to it that Jeffrey cooperates."

***

I have the United ticket I purchased earlier in the week for the New York shuttle, good for any flight. Leaving Quantico, I take a right onto I-95. Fortunately, at this time of day rush hour traffic is headed south. I park in the short-term parking at National. I am in the United boarding area within an hour after leaving Dillion. Flights are scheduled hourly on the hour. I make the three p.m. flight. A cab from JFK gets me to the office building where Jeffery works.

At a little before five, I'm standing in the reception area of a glass-encased forty-seven-floor office building, asking the receptionist to call my son-in-law's office. She's hesitant, but I tell her my visit is a birthday surprise. His wife is in the cab waiting at the curb. We plan to take him out to dinner. She smiles, buys into the story, calls his secretary, and tells her Mr. Portman has an important visitor in the lobby. He needs to come down to sign him in personally. I give her a conspiratorial smile and wait at the elevator bank.

A few minutes later Jeffrey steps out of the elevator. I take him by the elbow. "Jeffrey, keep smiling. We need to walk out the door, and I'll explain what is going on."

As we make it to the sidewalk and start walking, Jeffery somewhat shakily asks, "What the hell is going on?"

7

I lead him down the street into a small nondescript café. We grab a table, order coffee and sweet rolls, and I say, "Jeffery, to use a technical term, you're in deep doo-doo."

I recount to him my morning's visit at Quantico, Dillard's identifying Jeffery's visitor as Stanly Trocheck, and speculation as to Stanly's interest in Jeffery. We believe he is planning to launder money through Jeffery's accounts. I go on to tell him that the long-term prognosis for him is poor; he'll probably end up in prison for financial crimes.

But more importantly, my daughter and grandchildren are at risk. In thirty or 40 percent of cases like this, where the mob or cartel is involved, family members are assaulted, kidnapped, and some killed. I finish up by telling him, "You will cooperate with the FBI! You will work with them in a sting to bring Trocheck down. I will bring my resources to the party to help flush Trocheck into the open."

After initial reluctance, Jeffery agrees. "What do I do?"

3 The Plan

Later that week, I'm meeting with Colonel Anderson. I bring him up to speed with the FBI's findings. I tell him about Sydney Trocheck and his money laundering operation. "It appears Sydney is one of the mobs behind the scenes players, and Wanda and the twins may be in some danger." I finish up capsulizing my meeting with Jeffery. "Jeffery is freaked out, but he will work with the FBI. I told him that I was going to catch Sydney Trocheck."

"That was a rather bold promise," Anderson says.

"Colonel, I need a few weeks of leave."

Anderson setting his coffee mug down, says smugly, "I suggest you delay that. We have a new contract, and as a matter of fact, their man is bringing it by this morning for me to sign. I proposed you as our lead operative."

I start to speak, but Anderson raises his hand and continues with the details. "The contract is with the FBI. It's seeking our assistance in developing field practices to catch 'scumbags' like Trocheck. Agent Dillion will be here with the contract for me to sign. He asked that you be here."

Dillon arrives later that morning and is ushered into the Colonel's office. Anderson calls me in. Anderson is just putting his pen down as I walk in. "Okay Sean, we are now contracted with the FBI. Our first assignment is to develop procedures to capture money launderers. We thought Sydney Trocheck would make a good case study."

We spend the next hour or so discussing how to proceed and making tentative plans, knowing those plans will have a short shelf life once we start.

Dillion looks at me, "I'm assigning two agents to work with you, both with extensive field experience. The three of you will be going to Coeur d'Alene, Idaho; my agents will go next Thursday via Fairchild Air Force Base, and Sean, you will follow on Friday directly to Coeur d'Alene. We've booked you into the Coeur d'Alene Casino Resort Hotel. Sorry, it's only a three-star resort. Obviously, once you get there, you don't know each other. We have three days to build your background stories and get supporting papers. Comments, questions?"

"I'm fine for now," I say, "let's get started."

"One last thing," Dillion says, "stop shaving. We want you with facial hair since your face was in some publications last year after the Sa'd Ibn Atiq affair."

***

My new name is Alan Saul. I'm an accountant with a small pharmaceutical company. For years, I've been skimming money from my employer by buying ingredients from secondary Chinese sources and doctoring invoices to make it appear they were the best ingredients. Chemically there was no difference, but quality-wise, that is another matter.

As a sideline, I'd occasionally reroute drug shipments. I would then sell those shipments to an East Coast drug dealer. Sales would occur maybe three times a year and net me in the neighborhood of a hundred thousand dollars per sale. "Hey, what can I say? Quality drugs sell at a premium."

Charlie, my old money launderer, got snuffed when he got greedy with a drug kingpin's money. I need to move several hundred thousand dollars a year, small potatoes in the grand scheme of things, but when the money is in your pocket, so to speak, it is a big deal.

The FBI created my employment history going back a decade, supported by legitimate tax records. The coup de grâce is an offshore account in Panama with nearly a million dollars.

My FBI partners are assuming the identities of Air Force enlisted members stationed at Fairchild AFB. They are going to Coeur d'Alene for a few days of R&R. Both agents have substantial field experience. Oscar, the small one, is wiry and, I am told, has the disposition of a rabid dog when aroused. His specialty is financial forensics. The larger of the two, Jacob, is a black guy, perhaps pushing 250 pounds, without a trace of fat.

"Sean, good to meet you," said Jacob. "I'm impressed with your background. Dillion has been telling us stories, but I'm sure he must be exaggerating; North Korean spies, cartel drug lords, Islamic fanatics."

"Ah shucks," I say. Dillion must have his facts confused, "I was also on your most wanted list for a while."

11

And you, you look like a linebacker. Did you play professional ball?"

"I played a season with the Kansas City Chiefs. In college, I was the big dog in a small kennel. In the NFL ... well, let's just say I got tired of being ground into hamburger every week and opted to join the FBI where the worst that could happen was being shot."

Three days of not shaving gave me a new devil-may-care look. The horn-rimmed glasses, turns out I needed minor corrective lenses, gave me an intellectual flair.

In short, I was rebranded as a dashing crook.

Before I left, Dillon gave me a new cell phone, preprogrammed with various numbers, dry cleaner, restaurants, etc., as part of my cover. One of the speed dial numbers was a now disconnected number for my deceased business partner. Calling that number, followed by a select alphanumeric code, got me to Dillion.

I was ready!

5 Coeur d'Alene

I walk out of the Coeur d'Alene airport at about four-thirty. There is no courtesy hotel shuttle. I take the taxi at the head of the taxi queue. The driver, a young boy maybe from India, asks where to and I tell him the Casino Resort Hotel.

"Sahib," he starts, "it is not any of my business, but they are a den of thieves. Their games are rigged, and they renege on big payouts."

"What can you tell me about the people who run the casino."

"The Schitsu'umsh, the tribal name of the local Indians, have contracted with the Three Aces Management Company. Three Aces have their fingers into three or four other casinos in the state."

"Interesting," I say. We chat a bit longer, and I find him a fountain of information. He is not a casino supporter. He has a scholarship to North Idaho College, Sarah Palin's alma mater, where he is working toward an associate degree in physical therapy. His parents live in Spokane, immigrating to the US as children when Bangladesh broke away from Pakistan in the early 70s. As a Muslim, he is opposed to gambling and the sins it brings. He tells me his

13

'sahib routine' is good for larger tips. My gut has a good feeling about **Masum.**

In the hotel parking lot, I show him Sydney's 8X10. "Do you recognize this guy?"

"Yes, Sahib, he is a frequent face at the casino."

"What can you tell me about him?"

"Not much. He associates with bad men. Some from the Three Aces, others from the Indian tribe, and some Hispanics now and then. Probably drug dealers! I drove him home one night. He lives in a large house on the lake in Fernan Lake Village."

"Masum, give me your cell number. I will call if I need a ride," or other help, I add under my breath.

***

I'm having breakfast in the casino's restaurant the next morning as Jacob and Oscar pass through, oblivious to me. Looks like they are headed to the caddie shack, probably planning on a morning chasing a small white ball around the lush fields surrounding the casino complex. I've never gotten into golf. My few attempts proved embarrassing, especially when the young lady I was with beat me by twenty strokes. Jacob and Oscar hooked up with two seedy-looking characters for a foursome. Good, a little investigation, or were they just blending into the scenery?

After eating and a second cup of coffee, not particularly good coffee, I wandered around the casino. Watched the staff, located the casino's offices, and then toured the grounds. Given that only diehard gamblers were at the slots midmorning, the blackjack and roulette tables were not open. I blended in with the geriatrics wandering the grounds clearing their heads from the previous night. I was concerned I might become conspicuous hanging around the casino all day so I called Masum. Fifteen minutes later I was in Masum's taxi. "Masum, how about giving me a tour of Coeur d'Alene? I don't want to be back here until seven. Here is $500 for the day. Let's plan to finish up at a good steakhouse off the tourist track; I'll buy dinner."

"Sahib, I would be glad to be your tour guide for the day. But as I mentioned yesterday, I am a college student. I have a class this afternoon that I must attend. A mid-semester test that I'd prefer to skip but can't. It's one of my key courses."

"That's not a problem. Drop me off downtown in the shopping district. I'll browse around. I'll be lost for a couple hours if I can find a good used bookstore. But if you have other plans for the day, I can make other arrangements."

"No, no, your plan is excellent! I'll drop you off at Aladdin's Used Bookstore; it's in the shopping district and not far from the lakeside attractions."

Aladdin's Used Bookstore comprised two floors of used books. There was an attached café where one was encouraged to take a book. A number of books were laying on tables for customers to peruse while enjoying a croissant and coffee. The coffee was excellent.

I found three books I had to have; one was a history of the Army's Rangers. The cashier said I could have them mailed for a nominal charge. Great, what could go wrong? I gave her Anderson's home address. I would tell him later to expect them.

Later that afternoon Masum picked me up. It was getting close to dinner time. "Masum, let's find that restaurant and beat the evening rush."

"There is an excellent restaurant on the city's east side; not many tourists get out that way. It's the *Steak and Chips*. Best ribeye stake in Idaho."

The Steak and Chips surpassed Masum's description. One of the best steaks I've had.

Later returning to the casino, I thank him for the day. "Sahib, I feel guilty taking your money. Today was a break in my tedium."

"No, you earned it. I will call you again when I need your services," I said as I turned to walk into the casino's lobby, a transition from fresh air into a den of deceit.

"As I walk around the gaming tables, who do I see? None other than **Sydney Trocheck**."

6 Contact

Sydney's sitting at a blackjack table. I stand back and watch him for three or four hands. He's clearly a gambling novice, doesn't know what he is doing. The elderly lady beside Stanley gets up, plainly doing much better than Sydney, and I take her seat. I win the next three hands.

Sydney looks over and says, "You are lucky tonight."

"No," I say, just following my daddy's advice. "Play the table."

After a few more hands, I lose two, Stanley loses five. A bit disgusted he starts to get up.

"I think it's time for a break," I say, "let's get a drink."

We wander over to the lounge area; some nondescript comedian is on the stage that we ignore. "What's your daddy's advice?" Sydney asks.

"I usually sell this advice, but ... first, don't try to count face cards; the dealer uses at least four decks. Just keep in mind there are more numbered cards than face cards. If you see a run of face cards, there is a greater probability of a number card next in the stack. Second, that dealer was overly aggressive. He'd take a hit when he should have passed. You sit pat, let him go bust." After listing a few more observations, I say, "Let's go back and see how you do."

An hour later, Sydney pulls away from the table with a large stack of chips. The dealer is glad to see him go.

I get up, telling Sydney I have someplace I need to be. "Maybe our paths will cross tomorrow."

***

I'm just finishing my second cup of tolerable coffee the next morning while reading the newspaper in the hotel's café.

"Good morning, my friend," a voice says. "I didn't get your name yesterday evening, but that was the best I ever did at the blackjack table. Do you mind if I join you?"

"Please have a seat. I'm Alan Saul. And you are?"

"Sydney Trocheck"

I used an article in the paper to open a discussion on world politics; we drift into sports and, finally business. I comment, "You appear to have a firm grasp on the business world. Are you one of the wheeler and dealers?"

"No," he laughs, "just investments here and there."

"It's not entirely accidental I'm here. One of my business associates recently died. He's known in the trade simply as Charlie. Since his demise, I've been at a loss as to investment opportunities. I'm looking for a new investment counselor."

Sydney looks at me, "By any chance did Charlie die of unnatural causes?"

Somewhat cautiously, "I understand it was mob-induced lead poisoning. Apparently, he made some unwise investments for a New Jersey mob boss."

"Tell me more about yourself; what do you do?" says Sydney."

"Nothing that exciting. I'm an accountant at Kite Manufacturing, a subsidiary of Gilead Pharmaceuticals. Kite's principal focus is cell therapy manufacturing. We have several facilities. I'm located at the Frederick, Maryland facility, which has a small center that studies and produces new synthetic opium products for cancer treatment."

"And you are the accountant that oversees this center?"

"No, I'm the accountant that oversees all of the Frederick plant's business."

"Tell me," says Sydney with new interest, "was there some connection between your job at Kite and Charlie?"

"Possibly," I quietly respond.

After a few moments of contemplation, Sydney tells me he needs to make a few phone calls. It's possible he might be able to help me with a new investment counselor. He suggests we meet for breakfast tomorrow to continue our discussion.

***

Okay, it's not quite 10 a.m., so what do I do the rest of the day. About then I see Jacob and Oscar heading to the caddie shack. On impulse, I follow them. I asked the attendant if there was a group going out I could join.

"Not at this time. It's a slow morning. Come back this afternoon," the pimply boy says.

19

From behind me, Oscar pipes up, "You can join us if you would like to make up a threesome."

"Great" turning to the pimply boy, I ask to rent some clubs.

We get to the first tee, and I thoroughly embarrass myself with three mulligans. By the third hole, I'm up twenty-five strokes. Jacob in a low voice quips, "I hope you can shoot better than you play golf."

It takes me the next three holes to bring them up to speed on my meeting with Sydney. We agreed to meet at the buffet the following evening for a Sydney update. I also tell them of Masum, suggesting they keep a casual watch on him in the event I must use him for support.

To maintain cover, we play the remaining twelve holes. I shoot 133, Oscar 82, and Jacob 78. As I limp back to the caddie shack, I'm reminding myself why I hate golf! I decline their invitation to join them at the 19th hole.

7 The Setup

I spend the afternoon with a hot bath and a nap. Early that evening I joined the geriatric set in the buffet line. I helped an elderly lady in front of me with her tray, my god, she had an appetite and got her settled back at her table with her friends. "Thank you, young man," she says, "you remind me so much of my son. He died in Afghanistan several years ago."

With some compassion, I tell her I am sorry for her loss.

After fortifying myself with a generous dose of roast beef, I head to one of the gaming rooms. I claim a slot machine at the end of one of the many rows giving me a good view of the room. Blackjack tables to the left, crap tables to the right. The roulette wheels, usually the choice of the more sophisticated players, are in another room. I watch the pit bosses overseeing the tables. Occasionally calling for a cart with an armed guard to collect the growing stacks of the guests' donations. I never see a table run out of dealer chips. This is a profitable operation. I'm guessing all the profits are reported – right!! I'm thinking Sydney is in the thick of this, moving a portion of the profits into 'black' accounts.

After dropping a couple hundred quarters into the slots, I move on to the craps tables.

As my turn comes around, I try my luck with the dice. I'm soon on a winning streak. A bevy of young ladies materialize behind me, cheering me on. I let my bet ride and throw the dice. I get a cheer from my new supporters. I let it ride again, and more cheers. My third time, I attract the attention of one of the pit bosses. He's thinking I'm either very lucky or have slipped in loaded dice. He talks with one of the dealers at the table, exchanges the dice, and steps back.

My goal was to get their attention. I did that. I collect my chips, definitely putting a dent in that table's cash flow and cash out. My bevy of supporters follow me to the cashier's window. I tell the young ladies I have other business, thanking them for their enthusiasm and give each a hundred-dollar chip. My take, $57 thousand in cash and a couple thousand in chips for my next stop, the roulette tables. Not bad for an hour.

At the roulette table, I quickly reduce my horde of chips. Just for the hell of it, I put all my remaining chips on green. I doubled my holdings. I moved the growing stack of chips to a bet on even. Doubled again! In a final brazen move, I put the entire lot on 24. Why twenty-four? It was the number closes to me on the table. I had the room's attention. The croupier laughed. She spun the wheel and released the ball. Around and around it went. The ball settled on 24. The croupier was speechless, the other folks around the table awe-struck. I did a mental calculation. I started with about $900 and doubled it. I let that ride and doubled it again, bringing it to about $3,600 on the table. Hitting twenty-four multiplies my stake by thirty-five times the bet on the table. The croupier was looking at a payout of over $125,000. She called over the pit boss. He sized up the situation authorized the payout then escorted me to the cashier's window, where a check was cut in my name. Now, what does one do with a big check made out to an assumed name you are using for undercover work? I need Sydney's help.

***

Sydney is waiting for me when I walk into the breakfast café. I order eggs sunny side up, toast, bacon, and coffee. "Sydney aren't you eating," I ask.

"Already did; the waitress just cleared the table." He refills his coffee cup from the coffee carafe remaining on the table.

"After our talk yesterday, I did a little research," Sydney continues. "I talked with a couple of Charlie's compatriots. They had vague memories of you but agreed that Charlie moved funds for you three or four times a year. Definitely not a big operation."

"That's about right," I said. Now that Charlie is no longer with us, I have about a quarter million I need to move, more than I ever needed to move at any one time. Also, a check from the casino that I'd rather not report on my taxes."

"What is your normal annual cash flow."

"Normally a little less than a half million dollars a year," I respond.

Sydney looks at me, "I don't think I can help you. My clients move millions of dollars a year. Your enterprise is too small for the risks involved."

As he starts to get up, I continue. "Most of my funds originate from the sale of misdirected opioid shipments; a thousand pills in each shipment. I can usually misdirect three, maybe four shipments per year. Shipments are to an East Coast drug network and nets me about $10,000 per shipment. A fraction of the value of the product

23

and a high level of risk to me. Now I was thinking if I misdirected a shipment now and then to one of your customers, we could be talking millions of dollars."

"Stay here, have some more coffee. I'll be back shortly."

Sydney gets up and leaves the room. My two confederates enter the café. After a quick glance around, they take a table not far away. Sipping my coffee, I give them a subtle thumbs up, their sign to stick close.

Sydney returns and, not sitting down, says, "I have some friends that would like to talk to you." I get up, following him through one of the gaming rooms into the manager's office in the back.

I look around; there are three others in the room. Two apparently are muscle since they remain standing by the back wall. There is just a small round table with four chairs in the middle of the room, a computer desk on one wall, a lounge chair, and a bank of screens on the wall monitoring each of the gaming rooms. The only door is the one we entered by.

The third man, clearly the guy in charge, looks like an older casting reject from the Godfather. "Sydney here tells me you have an interesting proposition. You can provide us high-quality opioids."

"Yes," and I repeat the earlier story I told Sydney.

The 'Don' isn't excited about the deal; he wants more product. "You say you can only provide three, maybe four shipments per year. I want at least ten."

Looking him in the eye, "If you can put on a suit two sizes too small for you and walk around the casino without getting stares, I'll consider it. My shipment schedule is based on physical constraints. If I exceed them, the scheme collapses."

"Cheeky little bastard," he says. "Antonio, take him out to the Indian burying grounds."

The two goons come around the table; Antonio has small pistol in his hand, and they escort me out the door through the gaming room and into the parking lot.

I keep my right hand balled into a fist. One would think I'm ready for a fight, but that would be wrong. It is my signal to Jacob and Oscar it is time to activate plan 'B.'

8 Plan B

The two goons are giving me the bum's rush out of the casino. We are headed to a black limo on the far side of the parking lot. Jacob and Oscar quietly slip up behind "Hold it, they whisper," gun in one hand and FBI credentials in the other. They disarm my two new friends and slap handcuffs on them. "Okay, Alan, what now," Oscar asks.

"Let's take these two back into the casino and finish my talk with Angelo."

The gaming room is not particularly crowded this time of day, but we do get some stares. We bust into the manager's office, and Sydney and Angelo are still sitting at the table. Jacob settles the muscle on two chairs he places by the back wall. Oscar flashes his credentials and starts talking about a raid.

"Meet my associates," I start. "Some would call them rogue agents; I prefer to refer to them as agents of opportunity. Now, where were we? As I said, I can deliver three, maybe four deliveries of high-quality opioids per year. Before I was rudely cut off, there is a potential I can increase that to ten or fifteen deliveries. I am currently the chief accountant at the Frederick, Maryland, Kite facility. Big fish, small pond, if you get my drift. I'm in the running for a key position for one of Gilead's facilities in California. I would be a big fish in a big pond."

"Now I'm guessing you are not the big boss. I suspect he's listening in." Speaking to the hidden mike, "Now listen up, I'm offering you a sweet deal here. But if it's too big for you, I'll take it to a small casino I know in Wyoming. I understand they are your chief competitor in this market. I'm leaving a phone number with Sydney. Call me within forty-eight hours. After forty-eight hours, the number will be disconnected. One last bit of advice, don't let the greaser here screw up this deal."

I collect my rogue agents, and we leave the resort. We don't check out; just drive into the sunset metaphorically, that is, given its noontime. We packed anything important that morning into the car Oscar rented earlier as backup transportation. To ensure all ties with the resort were cut, we drove to the airport where Oscar returned the rental car at Hertz. At the same time, Jacob obtained another vehicle from a small rental company under a new FBI alias.

A couple days earlier, Jacob rented the top floor of a small boutique hotel, the Blackwell Hotel, not far from Fernan Lake Village. By three that afternoon, we were off the grid.

I left my team so they could do whatever FBI agents did and wandered toward the downtown area. I see Aladdin's Used Bookstore on the next block, so for the lack of any other plan, I go there. Sitting in its café reading an old sports tell-all book and sipping coffee, I decide to call Masum and ask him to meet me at the bookstore. Earlier, I had Anderson run a background check on him, and he is what he said he was. A poor student on a scholarship with immigrant parents from Bangladesh who now live in Spokane. No police record, and amazingly for a taxi driver, no traffic violations.

Twenty minutes later, Masum looks around the café for me, sees me, comes over, and sits at my table.

"Sahib, why aren't you at the gaming tables on such a nice day?"

"Masum, can I trust you? Do you want to make a little extra money?"

"Yes, and yes, if it is legal."

"Tell me about the Steak and Chips restaurant. When we were there, I noticed what appeared to be party rooms. Are they available to the public?"

"Yes, just call ahead, and you can reserve one. I think there is a small reservation fee, but party rooms are available to the public on a first-come basis."

"Earlier, you indicated you held Sydney in low esteem and had no use for casinos. I am running sting against both. If it works out, the casino will blame Sydney for the fed's intervention. My motive, Sydney attempted to screw my son-in-law, and I'm taking him down. What I need from you is reliable transportation. Nothing more."

"Nothing illegal on my part?" asks Masum.

"No, and you can walk anytime you feel uncomfortable."

"Okay," he says somewhat hesitantly.

"Masum, if you are in, I need to visit that restaurant now."

Twenty minutes later we are pulling into the Steak and Chips parking lot. There is parking for about twenty cars. The backside of the lot is bordered by a stand of pine trees. There is a small strip mall

28

on the other side of the street and a collection of small businesses down the street. Nothing threatening.

We go into the restaurant. Looking around, I see no obvious security threats, hiding places, etc. No security cameras. At the receptionist's desk, I make a reservation for one of the party rooms for the following evening. I ask for the one at the end of the hall, and can I take a quick look at it now? It's a midsized room, probably can handle twenty or so people. She asks, "How would you like it set up; one big table or multiple tables? I think we can do five."

"I think one large table. A rectangle down the center of the room."

Stepping out of the room, I notice an EXIT door immediately to my right.

"Is that door always locked?" I ask.

"Yes, the fire alarm goes off if it's opened."

As we return to her desk, I thanked her for her help and told her my party would be at about six tomorrow.

As Masum and I get back to his cab my cell rings.

"Is this Alan Saul?" a voice asks.

"Who am I talking to?"

"That's not important," the voice says.

I hang-up.

The phone rings again; I answer saying "Do you have a name yet?"

There is a pause, then the voice says, "Big Bear. I'm one of the casino trustees. We talked about your proposal and would like to proceed. Where can we meet? Here at the casino?"

"How about tomorrow night about six? As for meeting at the casino, no, I feel too vulnerable there. Let me suggest a neutral meeting spot, the Steak and Chips restaurant in east Coeur d'Alene. I believe they have some party rooms; I'll reserve one under my name. And let's restrict the number of attendees. Myself and my two rogue agents and on your side you, Sydney, and 'Don Corleone.' I'll walk if I see any additional bodies."

9 The Meeting

I have Masum drive me to the Blackwell Hotel.

"Sahib, you're staying here? I've never noticed it before."

"Park the car and come in with me. There are a couple guys you need to meet."

We go in, climb the winding staircase, and enter the suite of rooms. Jacob and Oscar look up. They look up, somewhat surprised, and ask who I have in tow.

"This is Masum, my ride. I thought I should introduce him so you won't shoot him in the crossfire."

Masum starts looking for the door as I add, "Just joking Masum. But seriously, you need to know each other. I told Masum about Sydney's attempt to screw my son-in-law and the fact I'm taking him down. I didn't mention the FBI's involvement."

"The FBI?" Masum mutters. Oscar pulls out his credentials. "This is an undercover operation, and it best stays that way. You don't breathe a word of this to anyone." Oscar says.

"Okay, now that we are all friends, we need a plan for tomorrow night." I tell Jacob and Oscar about my activities and Big Bear's call.

"We have a meeting tomorrow at six."

Looking at Jacob and Oscar, "We will drive over in the rental, getting there about five. There is a grove of pine trees we can hang out in while we monitor the restaurant. We'll let them go in first."

Masum, here is a hundred bucks. Why don't you take your girlfriend to an early dinner at the Steak and Chips? Get there about six but linger over your dinner until you see us leave. If I need a ride, which will be unlikely, you'll need to move rapidly. I suggest you prepay your bill and then linger over dessert.

As Masum starts to leave, I walk out with him, handing him some cash. I hope this meets your expectations, and we will talk later.

Jacob is all over me when I go back in. "What are you doing bringing in a civilian? What do you know about him? Can he be trusted?" and so forth.

"I met Masum when I first got here, got his story, and had Colonel Anderson check him out. Dillion ran his name through your database. He is vetted. Masum is a student, is plugged into local gossip, and can provide discrete transportation. We can trust him" I say in his defense.

"Okay, but I don't like it," Jacob sputters.

**

We pull into the restaurant parking lot at quarter to five. Jacob parks the car on the backside of the lot next to the employees' vehicles trying to blend in. It's a pleasant day, so it's not unpleasant hanging out in the patch of trees. Sitting on the pine needles behind a downed tree renders us almost invisible from the parking lot, especially as dusk sets in.

32

Masum and a cute young lady arrive shortly before six. I notice he parks so he can make a quick getaway if needed.

Shortly after six, a casino SUV pulls into the lot; three men get out and go into the restaurant. "My god, nothing like being subtle, is there" Oscar exclaims as he eyes their vehicle.

We follow them in.

If stares could kill Angelo's would have me six feet under; he was clearly not a happy camper. Big Bear was in charge of their delegation. He beats me to opening remarks. "Alan, this is a delightful restaurant. As a visitor to our city, how did you find it?"

"I asked a store clerk downtown to recommend a good steak. She pointed me in this direction. I recommend the house special, a ribeye steak. But enough chit-chat; let's get down to business. My offer still stands. Today I can deliver five thousand pills per shipment, three, maybe four shipments per year. I've been dealing with East Coast dealers netting $100K per shipment. This is a high-risk operation for me. If I could reduce risk, I could see myself settling for $80K per shipment.

"Well, we offer you little risk," says Big Bear. I suggest eight dollars per pill. And that is with the understanding we can expect more frequent deliveries once you get your promotion."

After a short, thoughtful pause, "I could work with ten per pill."

"Nine," says Big Bear.

"This is close to robbery," I say but we can start with that.

Big Bear continues, "How do we know what kind of quality product we will be getting, and when can we expect our first delivery?"

"Two weeks from this Friday. In the meantime, I will get you a small introductory sample this Friday. Two hundred pills, no charge. Where do you want them shipped to? The casino? The reservation? The Don's home address?"

"We thought you'd deliver them," says the Don.

"No, I'm not in the delivery business. But here is an idea, while you guys get your reception area set up, I'll schedule a one time delivery to Sydney at Sydney's home, FedEx, this Friday."

Sydney starts to object, but Big Bear says, "That will work."

"Well, now that is all settled, how about we eat? I've taken the liberty," I say, "to order dinner for us. The waitstaff is waiting to bring the food in."

10 Free Samples

After a good dinner and a few bottles of wine, Big Bear was in a friendly disposition telling us about his childhood on the reservation. He felt he was always seen as a second-class citizen, just as a backdrop for the tourists. In the winter, many young men like him worked the ski resorts, mostly in the background.

As a young man, he watched other tribes open casinos. A Foxwood-type casino became an obsession. He convinced the tribe's elders of the benefits a casino could provide the tribe but was stymied by the Bureau of Indian Affairs. There was one old bureaucrat who was convinced casinos were the ruin and damnation of Indian tribes. He would not tolerate them on 'his' reservations.

"I decided to sideline him," said Big Bear. "I hired a private investigator to look into his past. And guess what I found? Over a span of fifty years, he maintained three families on 'his' reservations.' Between them, he had eleven children and two grandkids. Running Fox and I paid him a visit in the White Man's capital. I told him I wanted a casino in Coeur d'Alene. He objected as I knew he would. I then told him I knew of his 'families' and thought the public would be interested. I started to dial the Washington Post. Before I punched in the last number, he agreed. He is now a big casino supporter as you can tell by the number he has approved in Idaho."

After a convivial evening, we went our separate ways. Oscar and Jacob were outside with Sydney enjoying Sydney's cigars. As I walked through the main dining room, I saw Masum and was tempted to go over and talk with him. I caught his eye and gave him a thumbs up and kept walking.

***

Early Friday, I take my 'spy' gear and set up a blind on the far side of Fernan Lake. It's in a woody setting, on a slight rise directly across from Sydney's home. He would not see it unless he was looking for it. And from this vantage point, I could get clear photos of the FedEx delivery of the freebies being delivered. In addition, the FedEx deliveryman was an FBI agent. The FBI was providing the two hundred pills from confiscated drugs and wanted to maintain control over the product for as long as possible.

The FedEx truck arrived at 11:13 a.m. Unknown to him at the time, Sydney was documented receiving the shipment.

Shortly after the truck was out of sight, Sydney is heading for the casino in his car. He's on his phone asking Angelo where he wants the opioids.

"Take them to the garage in back of the casino. Jimmy will meet you there."

Twenty minutes later, Sydney pulls up and, taking the package, enters the garage.

"You're busted," says a deep voice. Sydney's heart skips a couple beats and Angelo starts laughing, "Gotcha," he says.

"You bastard," squeals Sydney, "I almost had a heart attack."

"Okay, let's see what we have here," says Angelo as he takes the package, places it on the table, and opens it." There are forty pill containers, each with five pills, prescription size. "Convenient," says the Don, "we can sell these for seventy-five or a hundred dollars each, no repackaging.

"Get Bennie from the caddie shack and let him sample a pill or two," Angelo says. "Need to assess the quality of the product,"

Sydney pipes up, "Just give him one; we don't know how potent they are. Big Bear will be pissed if we kill him."

Jimmy returns in a few minutes with Bennie who is complaining about being dragged away from the caddie shack.

"We got a treat for you Bennie," Sydney says. "Try one of these pills."

After fifteen minutes, Bennie has zoned out; he has found his own groove. Two hours later, Angelo asks Bennie, who is just returning to reality, "How is that shit?"

"Man, that is the best stuff I've had in a long time. Can I get more?"

"You're going to be selling it, fifteen dollars a pop. And you will lose a finger for each pill you can't account for." Angelo picks up three vials and consolidates the contents into one. "Here are fifteen little beauties. I expect two hundred and fifty dollars by the end of the day. Good luck."

As Bennie wanders back to the caddie shack, Angelo says to Sydney, "Big Bear wanted a test of the product. Let's see how this works out."

That evening as the caddie shack is closing, Angelo is talking to Bennie. "How were sales?"

37

"Slow at first until word of mouth kicked in. I'm sold out and have a growing clientele. Is this going to be permanent?"

"Yes, but not at the caddie shack; too much a risk for the Casino."

11 The Operation

Jimmy, as the head of the Cacino's drug distribution center, reports to Angelo. The distribution center is in a small house the reservation owns, not far from the casino. It is off the main road, surrounded by pine trees. Angelo and Alan finally agreed that the drug shipments would go to the distribution center.

Five people work the drugs. Three runners who make deliveries and a packager. Jimmy oversees the operation and interfaces with the dealers. The center does not sell to individuals, just dealers. There are currently seven dealers in the Coeur d'Alene area. Product is normally provided by the Mexican cartel. It can be ordered as needed.

Alan's first shipment of opioids is scheduled for this coming Friday. It is small and will be infrequent, at least for now. It cuts into the cartel's business, and they will be pissed. Angelo sympathizes with the cartel, but Big Bear is the boss. Alan's sample shipment was clearly a better product than the cartels. Oh well, thinks Angelo, they can fight it out.

Friday morning Angelo and Alan are at the center waiting for the delivery truck. A nondescript panel truck approaches the farmhouse.

Angelo's men stop it, and as the driver steps out, the guards check for other passengers. All is good; they wave it forward. The van's side doors are opened, and Jimmy's people collect a medium-sized cardboard box. Angelo holds the truck there until Jimmy can get the delivery into the workroom and opens it to check its contents. All is good; the truck is allowed to leave.

Inside the box are four plastic bags, each containing hundreds of tablets.

"Alan," Angelo says, "your sample had the pills in small vials; now you just give us bags of tablets?"

"You want us to package the product for you?" Alan responds. Not a problem, there will be a 20 percent packaging charge."

Big Bear materializes from the back of the room and asks Jimmy, "Are these the same as the sample?"

"They look it. We can get Bennie to test them."

"No, we'll find out soon enough."

"Alan looks like we are off to a good start. When can we expect the next shipment?" he asks.

"As I explained earlier, the best I can do now is four shipments a year, so mark your calendar three months from today. I plan to be in my new job by the end of the year; we can plan monthly shipments then."

I turn to Big Bear, "Big Bear aren't you forgetting something, six thousand dollars."

12 Busted

Big Bear picks up a briefcase "Here you go; count it if you like ... Mr. Murphy."

"What?"

A Hispanic comes into the room at Big Bear's beckoning. He's a good-sized guy with a mean expression. "Gonzales here claims to be El Honcho's nephew. You know the name, don't you Sean?" asks Big Bear.

"Gonzales, tell Mr. Murphy your story."

"A couple of years ago, we were bringing a shipment of product into Texas. The DEA ambushed us. My Uncle, two security guards, and I broke free and headed back to the border. This scumbag was blocking our way. As they started shooting, I hid in the bushes, the other three made it across the river. Louis was hit. I was no more than ten feet from Murphy when he and his men lit out after my Uncle."

"I've spent the past two years looking for Murphy. I got his name from a local paper reporting the drug seizure. I confirmed it from my DEA sources. Yesterday I was in the casino meeting with Angelo checking on arrangements for our next delivery, and who did

I see? Mr. Murphy schmoozing with your money mover." My Uncle, El Honcho as Murphy likes to call him, is offering a reward for Murphy's head. Big Bear, your people can have the reward; I just want to take his head."

"An interesting story, don't you think Mr. Murphy? I had my people do a little online research, and guess what I found? An old story in a San Antonio newspaper, with your picture corroborating my friend's story."

Gonzales turns to Big Bear. "We've had a productive relationship for several years, and now I find you looking for new suppliers? I think it might be time to review our agreement, maybe realign delivery schedules and prices. The level of risk has increased. I find your money man talking with a known fed. What information has been leaked? What about the other tribes you represent? We have a problem here!"

Gonzales stands in front of me and plants his fist in my midsection. I double over and do my best not to vomit.

"Greetings from El Honcho," says Gonzales as he prepares to continue the assault.

Big Bear steps in. "I told you; you can have him once we are done here. I don't want Murphy's blood in the floorboards." He then turns to me. "Where are you friends" as he smacks me upside the head with his pistol. The chair I've just been tied to topples over.

As if on cue, windows shatter as flash bangs flew through them. The front door disintegrates as three heavily armed men in tactical gear burst into the room. Jimmy's last action was reaching for his pistol. Gonzales breaks for the back room, pistol in hand.

■■■

Apparently Big Bear and Angelo have been through this exercise before. They drop their weapons and stand with their hands above their heads. Jacob comes in and slaps cuffs on them.

Jacob rights my chair and cuts the rope binding me. "Sean, what the hell? You've blown our cover. When you didn't come out as planned, I moved up our timeline. By the way, you look like hell; your head is bleeding."

"Where's that bastard Gonzales." I wheezed, "He's the one who screwed the pooch on this operation."

"You mean the greaser who ran out the back door? He took a potshot at one of our men and disappeared into the woods."

I look around and see Big Bear's pistol lying in the corner. As I pick it up, Jacob says, "Don't do it Sean; he's not worth it."

With pistol in hand, I walk up to Big Bear and smack him upside his head with it. "That felt good," I exclaim and hand the pistol to Jacob. "What did you think, I was going to shoot him? Just a little payback."

■■■

13 The Snitch

We arrive back at the Blackwell Hotel in midafternoon. I disconnect my hidden camera. Damn, they make things small these days. The lens was a shirt button. You would never know it was a camera lens unless you saw the wire coming off its back and running down to my belt buckle, the recording device. This little sucker could record video for up to twelve hours. The mic was built into the buckle. Gonzales's punch had not harmed the camera or mic.

"Where is Oscar," I ask.

"Oscar is watching Sydney's home. We don't want him to bolt."

By dinner time that night, we were having a heart-to-heart talk with Sydney. "Sydney, we have a deal you can't refuse. I shaded the truth earlier about Jacob and Oscar being rogue FBI agents. They are top-notch agents and are here to take you in. They've been on your case for the past two years for money laundering. While that charge is still in the air, we also have you for drug distribution," I say as I lay out a half dozen photos of Sydney receiving the FedEx package.

Jacob picks up on squeezing Sydney. "Now the question is do you want to be charged with drug crimes, or would you prefer to help us sort out the casino's money laundering operation? For the former, you'll get a hard 15 to 20 years. For the latter, we can work out a deal where you get minimum time. You might be back on the street in 2 to 3 years. To help you in making your decision, I should tell you we just busted the casino's drug operation. It's only a matter of time before Big Bear turns on you. So why don't you join our team and beat him to the punch."

Local law enforcement has no authority on the reservation, but the FBI does. Oscar had been working with the Federal Judge in Boise for the past week and had his search warrant in hand. The four of us, Sydney has joined our team, head to the casino. We also brought along a five-member federal SWAT team. Over the protest of casino guards, and the amazed faces of the crowd, we secured the business office. Sydney led us to a small office accessible through a janitor's closet where the real financial records were kept.

It was hard closing the casino. Seniors howled in protest. One elderly lady had to be pried from 'her' slot machine; it was ready to payout she kept screaming. The tribal police were called in to help keep some order.

We stripped the place of all financial records and computers. The pit bosses were directed to collect all chips at the tables and bring them to the cashier's office. We commandeered two tribal police officers and put them in charge of the cashier's office, telling them they would be liable for any shrinkage.

Our last act before leaving was to call the tribal elders and turn over the casino keys to them.

We took the seized evidence to the FBI's remote processing center, an empty hangar on Fairchild Air Force Base. We had a long night going through it. Sydney was invaluable. He was able to quickly sort the cash flow from drugs, the skimmed profits, and the legitimate casino operations.

As Gonzales alluded, other tribes were laundering skimmed profits through the Coeur d'Alene casino. A sizable amount of profits.

Before heading back to the hotel for some sleep, Oscar called the Federal Judge in Boise to report the outcome of the raid. The judge took in the information, then asked Oscar to come to Boise the next day where he planned a meeting with the State's gaming Commission, the federal representative of the Bureau of Indian Affairs, and the head of the FBI's field office.

Now the big fish.

14 Jeffery

Jeffery, the father of my grandchildren. Jeffery Portman had a troubled childhood. His father disappeared when he was a toddler. His mother worked menial jobs to care for him and his older brother Billy. There were stints on welfare to cover gaps in her employment. Billy was three years older than Jeffery. Jeffery did well in school; it was his refuge. Billy, on the other hand, did well as the neighborhood-wise guy.

In his early teens, Billy joined a local gang. He was dead before he turned eighteen. He and his buddies attempted to carjack a new SUV at a gas pump. Unfortunately, there was a middle-aged lady in the passenger seat. Her husband had stepped out to work the gas pump on the other side of the vehicle. And doubly unfortunate for the carjackers, he was an armed homicide detective. One of the carjackers had a pistol. When all was said and done, there were two bodies on the ground, one being Billy.

Jeffery did well in high school and earned a scholarship to the state university. He excelled in his studies, majoring in economics and finance. His adviser recommended he stay for another year or two and take some graduate classes. During this time, he met Wanda Murphy. She was an undergraduate in the economics department.

47

Jeffery was a student instructor for some of her classes. Two years later, after both had graduated, Wanda with a Bachelor of Science in Economics, and Jeffery with a Master's, were married. The twins came three years after that.

Jeffery landed a prize job with a prestigious New York investment firm. Over time he became the financial adviser for several large accounts. He did good, steering those accounts into investments that made above-average returns. He did too good.

In his fifth or sixth year with the firm, he and his boss, Jeb Wilson, were invited to lunch at an exclusive restaurant with two men. Jeffery would later learn that they were senior East Coast Mafia. The purpose of the meeting was to open new accounts Jeffery would manage. Accounts that would be off the books. There was also a smattering of Caribbean bank accounts he would manage. Before details were fully spelled out, his boss and the two new clients told Jeffery he could walk away before becoming a player. Everything he had just heard never happened. Or if he stayed, he should be prepared to make serious money. Jeffery chose the money.

Over the next couple of years, Jeffery became quite adept at moving and hiding large amounts of money. During this time, he established a small business on the side. It was a small company he used to move and protect his funds. It was funded in part by fees earned from his new accounts. But the greater portion was attributed to his investment strategies. He established an account in Switzerland to hold the bulk of the funds. Wanda knew nothing of this account but was listed as a co-owner.

Sydney's arrival on the scene caused Jeffery great concern. If he told his clients he was being blackmailed, would he be a liability?

Would Wanda and the twins be in danger? He knew his father-in-law, Sean Murphy, worked for a 'spook' organization that managed off-the-book operations for the alphabet agencies. He also knew Sean had a knack for solving problems with 'bad' people.

Jeffery chose to enlist Sean's support, emphasizing the need for discretion.

15 The Turning

Back at the Blackwell Hotel, I take Sydney aside.

"What can you tell me about Jeffery Portman?" I ask.

"Jeffery," mimics Sydney.

"You know the poor schmuck you lured to Foxwood, where you hacked his laptop and gained access to his business files. The guy you intimidated by moving mob money into my grandchildren's accounts. The guy you wanted to be a front for you as you skimmed the mob's money."

I think it was the mention of my grandchildren's accounts when Sydney became more attentive.

"Sydney, here is what you're going to do," I said. "You are going to help us take down the mob. Well, maybe not a takedown, but empty their hidden accounts."

"No way in hell am I getting involved with that. That would be my death sentence," yelps Sydney.

Jacob steps in. "Sydney, you did good in helping us with the casino, and as we promised, we will be recommending a very light sentence for your hacking and manipulation of Jeffery's accounts.

But that recommendation will detail how you moved money out of the mob's accounts to squeeze Jeffery."

"This is blackmail," mutters Sydney.

"Yes, but good blackmail," I say. "Now, are you in, or do you want to take your chances in prison? I understand the mob's reach includes our most secure prisons."

***

We have a quiet flight back to New York. A little chit-chat formulating a plan. Once there, we are whisked away to a nondescript office in Manhattan, where Dillion meets us.

"Congratulations on Coeur d'Alene and on turning Sydney," Dillion says. The Department of Interior is in an uproar questioning its oversight of casino operations on tribal lands. They and the Treasury Department are talking about a joint task force. I suspect this talk will fade away as they determine the scope of the problem and whose fingers are in the pot."

It's late in the day when the FBI approach Jeffery as he leaves his office and is walking across the plaza. The agents invite him to a meeting. He is initially reluctant until Dillion's name is mentioned. He silently accompanies them.

As Jeffery enters the conference room, he sees Sean and Dillion at one end of the table. He goes over and takes a chair beside them.

"What's going on?" he asks."

"See that man in the light blue suit at the far side of the room," Sean asks. "You should recognize him. That's Sydney, the man who attempted to blackmail you. Turns out he has some interesting ties to the mob. He launders money for them. He knows their deepest financial secrets. Jeffery, is there anything you'd like to tell me?"

"Like what?"

"Oh, maybe you could tell us about the accounts you manage for the mob. The source of the cash flow going into the accounts. Small things like that. But first, let's watch the presentation the District Attorney has put together that describes the mob's finances."

After a two-hour PowerPoint presentation, most attendees wander off to do better things; after all, it's almost happy hour. My small group remains.

Dillion starts. "Jeffery, we want you to flip and work with us to bring the East Coast mob down."

"Why would I do that? I don't know anything."

"Well, that is not entirely true is it, Jeffery" Dillion says as he continues. "Sydney has documented your transactions with certain foreign banks for the past year. On a cursory review, we've taken some of Sydney's information and matched it up with data we've collected. In short, you're good for 10 to 15 years for illicit financial transactions and possible terrorist transactions, which will double the sentence.

"Should we talk?"

After several minutes Jeffery looks at me "Okay, I'll cooperate, but first, once this starts and they figure out I flipped, which they will, I need to ensure the protection of my family. They will be reprisal targets."

"I'll take care of Wanda and the twins," I promised.

It's late in the day, but Dillion wants to get a few things nailed down. He calls in one of the FBI's financial forensic investigators, a young lady about Wanda's age, and asks Sydney and Jeffery to join them. They spend the next hour comparing notes and roughing out a plan. They are running out of steam at about nine and agree to resume the next morning.

Not that we don't trust Sydney, Jacob accompanies him to FBI provided quarters ... a two-star hotel where the FBI has secured the floor.

***

I leave with Jeffery. We take a taxi to his upper westside brownstone, talking very little on the way. As we enter, I ask if he wants to tell Wanda what is going on or should I. He defers to me.

As we enter, Wanda meets us and, in a cheerful voice, "Dad, what are you doing here? Jeffery didn't tell me you were in town. Have you eaten? Let me call out for some Chinese."

"Wanda, we need to talk. First, where are the kids?"

"Upstairs doing their homework. Why?"

"Jeffery has a small problem. It started with your trip to Foxwood" ... and I explained the details up through his visit with me three weeks ago requesting help.

"Some of the accounts Jeffery manages belong to the East Coast Mafia. The degree of his culpability is debatable, but nevertheless, the FBI will be charging him with money laundering crimes."

"Jeffery!" she cries, "what the hell have you done?"

Jeffery holds up his hand and asks that I be heard out.

I continue, "The FBI is setting up an operation to take down the mob. Jeffery has been asked to help, with a promise of reduced charges. He's agreed."

Wanda is fuming at this point. "Dad, the twins were kidnapped a few years ago because the North Koreans were after you. Last year you made me and the kids targets for terrorists. Now my husband is setting me up for the mob. I can't believe it. Why can't I have a normal life."

Somewhat unwisely, I said, "But it's not boring is it?" If looks could kill.

As she regains some composure, and I'm surprised the kids haven't made an appearance due to the noise, I continue, "Dillion, you remember him, don't you, is proposing we move you and the kids into protective FBI custody. I told him I would handle this. You're, and the twins' safety is my first concern."

She finally calms down, and after a little more talk, we have a plan. "While I make arrangements, you will tell the neighbors you're going to Florida for the week, an unexpected invitation from an old school friend that can't be turned down. The friend has stage four cancer, and time is running out. Arnold and Millie will be going with you."

You need to visit the kids' school tomorrow, make arrangements for online classes and collect whatever material the teachers want them to have. An Eyeball security specialist, probably Mark, will be here in the morning to escort you and the kids."

"Mark," Wanda says, "wasn't he my escort last year when we were evading terrorists?"

"Yes," I say, "but you need to get all this done tomorrow. We will be leaving Thursday morning.

"To where?" she asks.

16 Hiding in Plain Sight

After a four-hour flight, we land at Crater Lake Regional Airport in the middle of the night. Anderson has loaned us Eyeball's Gulfstream so there is no record of Wanda's movement. Under my alias, Alan Saul, I rented a large SUV from National Car Rental. The vehicle is waiting for us when we touch down.

Mark checks it out and then helps load the luggage. Then we are off. Mark is driving, Wanda and the twins are sitting in the back. Before long, the twins are asleep.

"Okay dad, where are we, and where are we going?" Wanda asks.

"We're in Oregon and are going to Lakeview. And before you bring up our little excitement on our last visit, I figure this is the safest place I can put you and my grandkids. Amanda will be monitoring you guys; Rossie will alert Amanda to any new people she sees at Flo's. And the FBI has a safe house that comes with two resident agents."

"Mark, I even have a surprise for you. How would you like to be a deputy sheriff? I've made arrangements with the Sheriff for her to take you on as deputy sheriff. Your primary duties will be to augment her staff for Wanda's security. To maintain appearances, you will also be expected to do a little sheriffing work. You'll like it!"

After an hour's drive, we are in downtown Lakeview. The streets are empty, or more accurately, the town's main drag is dead. I see only one gas station open. Partway through town we take a left and drive up into the foothills that make up the east side of the town. After a 10-minute climb, Mark turns into a driveway leading to a nice, very nice log cabin. The circular driveway could accommodate four, maybe five cars. I get out and motion to Wanda to follow me up the steps onto the porch. The view is spectacular, overlooking the town and the valley beyond. I lived here for six months when I was masquerading as Dr. Hasgrow. But that's another story.

I knock on the front door, and after some rustling inside, it's opened by a middle-aged gent, perhaps in his late 50s.

"We've been expecting you; Dillion called yesterday. You must be Sean, and the young lady is Wanda. Where are the kids? Enough of my babbling come in."

The great room is as I remembered it. Large overstuffed leather furniture, a massive stone fireplace, and a gourmet kitchen off to the left of the open floor plan.

Wanda gets the kids out of the SUV. They needed to be awakened. Groggily, they follow her up the steps into the house, where a middle-aged woman descends on them.

"And these must be Millie and Arnold," she says. I'm sorry; let me introduce myself. I'm Nellie Eames, and he is Scott Eames, my husband. We are both semi-retired FBI agents. We manage this safe house for the Bureau. Two years ago, or thereabouts, an acting Sheriff recommended the FBI lease this property. They did, and we have been its custodians ever since. You are the first family we've hosted. We usually get informants, mostly single men, who are being sequestered until they testify."

Mark is bringing in the last suitcase and catches the last of Nellie's introduction. "Sean, isn't this where you lived when you were on the run?" Now that got the Eames's attention.

"Okay, to come clean several years ago, I lived here for six months. I was evicted when the city acquired the property as part of the original owner's estate. The Mayor's idea was to sell the property; the value then was a little north of $2 million and use the proceeds to fund the new doctor's salary. The house was sold to a lawyer from Eugene. He used it as a 'love nest.' His wife learned about it, and in the resulting divorce, he defaulted on the mortgage. The house reverted to the town. At the time, I was the acting sheriff and suggested to Dillion this would make a good safe house. The FBI leased the property, and apparently, it was a success. I'll fill in the rest of the story over coffee in the morning."

"Taking the hint, you folks must be exhausted," Scott interjects. "Let's get you to bed. There are three bedrooms upstairs. Nellie, can you take care of Wanda and the kids? Sean, Mark, you get the sofas. There are pillows and blankets in that closet," pointing to a door near the base of the stairs. "We can continue our talk in the morning."

***

Morning came much too soon. Mark was still sprawled out on one of the couches, snoring loudly. It's a wonder anyone could sleep. I found the coffee pot, a good old fashion percolator, and started a pot. I found some pastries in the fridge, along with bacon and eggs.

I had breakfast well underway when Scott emerged from the master suite that's tucked away in back of the great room. "I thought I smelled bacon. Nellie will be out shortly."

A few minutes later, the three of us were sitting at the table with our coffee. Nellie starts telling me about them. "Scott and I were field agents for twenty years. Counter to FBI policy, we've been married for the last ten. Three years ago, we decided to retire; we were both in good health and wanted to enjoy life. Dillion had a deal we couldn't refuse. That's an overused phrase, but it was a good deal. We'd manage this house babysitting occasional 'clients.' He'd make sure we have at least several weeks a year with no clients so we can travel. And the best part, we enjoy a scenic rent-free setting."

She continues, "Now, to set your mind at ease, we are still fully functioning agents. Wanda and your grandkids will be well protected. This house has the latest security systems installed. No one will get within fifty yards of the house without us knowing. The doors and windows are reinforced, and we have a modest armory on site. Dillion tells us you work for a security firm and we should give you a complete tour. You may have some recommendations for improvement. Scott will give you a tour later this morning, but in the meantime ......"

Arnold is bounding down the stairs. "Grandpa, where are we? What's for breakfast?"

"Well, you're on the right track," I say. "Here's some scrambled eggs and bacon, and don't tell your mother, a danish."

58

"Don't tell your mother what?" Wanda says as she comes down the stairs.

"I'm corrupting your son with pastries," I say as I pour her a cup of coffee and place a danish in front of her.

Wanda rolls her eyes as she takes a bite.

"Scott, I'll take you up on your tour later, but first, Mark and I have some people to see."

Mark is up and moving as I push him out the door. Our first stop is Flo's where Mark gets the lumberman's breakfast, and I settle for coffee. Rossie is surprised to see me; it's been about two years since I was there.

"What is it this time, Sean? You've been a doctor, a sheriff, now what a spy chaser?" Rossie quips.

"No nothing that exciting, just bringing down the mob."

"You're kidding, right?"

"Not totally. My daughter and grandkids are staying up at Dr. Hasgrow's old house with an FBI protection detail. You might say they are in hiding. I need to ask a favor of you. If you see any strangers in town, please tell Amanda immediately. If she's not there, call Mark; he's her new deputy sheriff" I say as I give her a card and point to Mark while he is wolfing down his food. "I expect he will become one of your better customers."

"Mark will be an acting deputy helping Amanda with Wanda's security workload."

Our next stop is the sheriff's office. Amanda is expecting us. The Mayor appointed her sheriff when the previous sheriff, Samuel

Horneck, moved back to Israel and just after my temporary sojourn as the acting sheriff.

"I've made arrangements with Agent Dillion," she says. "Is this my new deputy?" She probably has Mark beat by ten years; she is clearly in charge.

"Yes, he's one of my rottweilers. I'll tell you the story someday. He can be relied on; he was with Samuel and me on our Texas and Iraqi adventures. He can exaggerate over a beer some night."

After a short review of the tasks at hand, I head back to the safehouse leaving Mark in Amanda's care.

At the safe house, Scott gives me the tour. It is impressive, and I have no suggestions for improvement. I spend a little time with Wanda and the kids, assuring them Jeffery will be fine and to treat this as a vacation, an extended vacation.

I ask Scott to take me to Lakeview's airfield in the rented SUV where the Eyeball Gulfstream waits. Later he will return the SUV to the Crater Lake Regional Airport car rental facility. There is no record as to where Wanda and the kids are.

16 Playing with Fire

As Wanda and the kids were moving to a more secure setting, Dillion has Jeffery and Sydney sequestered in a downtown office, planning their strategy for a financial attack on the East Coast mob.

"Jeffery," Dillion starts, "how does the mob interact with you? How do they get money to you? What do you normally do with it?"

"Normally I'll get a text telling me of a new deposit in one of five accounts. The text specifies which account. These accounts, except for one, are accounts with the institution where I am a senior financial manager. The fifth account belongs to BOFA. I'll transfer these new deposits to a special account I established for this purpose. This account is not reflected in the bank records; you must dig deep to get to it. Accounts of this type normally support CIA or FBI covert operations and need a senior bank vice president's approval. Jeb Wilson, vice president for internal management, provided the approval."

Dillion interrupts, "This Jeb Wilson works with various federal agencies?"

"Yes," responds Jeffery. "Now, getting on with the cash flow, I normally let the funds sit in this account for a few days, commingling with other deposits to ensure there is no electronic trace on them. On the third day, I transfer the funds to an account in Panama. From there I direct it to one of three numbered accounts, two in the Caribbean and one in Switzerland."

"On infrequent occasions, a mob courier will bring me a briefcase with money, usually a couple hundred thousand dollars. This is problematic. How do I take this much cash and ask a teller to deposit it? There are federal reporting requirements. The procedure we worked out was a quick trip to Panama. The mob will provide me an escort. Leaving the country is not a problem; entering Panama requires a little bribery. My escort takes care of that. A short taxi ride to the Banco la Hacienda, a private meeting with the bank director, and the money is deposited. Juan, the bank director, will then invite us to lunch at his club. And I'm back home in time for a good night's sleep."

Sydney's been sitting listening. "Here are a couple ideas. First, if I knew when the money is being moved to Banco la Hacienda, I could intercept the transfer and direct it elsewhere. The downside, this will put Jeffery at risk. A more elegant and difficult approach is to attack when the money is being transferred from Banco la Hacienda to one of the numbered accounts. The money leaves Panama and …. disappears."

"Jeffery, what is the elapsed time between your moving the money to Panama and its movement to a numbered account? asks Sydney.

"It's normally moved within twenty-four hours."

"If we put a tap on the Banco de la Hacienda's account, I could intercept the transfer as it's being made," Sydney says. "But I'll I need help with this; it's beyond my skill set."

"I think I can get you that help," says Dillion. "Now, this plan stops their money flow. Two issues remain, draining the mob's accounts of all funds and enticing mob players out of the woodwork."

"I can remove all funds from those accounts anytime you like. All I need are the passwords," Sydney says, looking at Jeffery.

"I guess I'm the bait," says Jeffery. "Once money starts disappearing, I'll be the mob's first suspect."

***

Three days later, Dillion gets a call from Jeffery. "I just received a briefcase with a million dollars in cash. The mob has scheduled my trip to Panama tomorrow."

"Okay, go with the flow. I'll alert Sydney."

Jeffery and his escort go to Teterboro Airport the following morning, board a small plane, and are at the Banco la Hacienda by 2 p.m. He called ahead, and Juan was expecting them. Juan takes the briefcase, counts the money with Jeffery and his minder, doesn't want any misunderstandings, and then has his teller deposit it. Jeffery suggests the money should be transferred to Switzerland sooner rather than later.

As is customary, Juan invites them to a late lunch. As they are finishing coffee and sweets, Juan's cell rings. He excuses himself and, standing away from the table, takes the call. The poor man, he's in his 60's, almost has a heart attack.

Stumbling back into his chair, he gasps, "Your money disappeared as we were transferring it!"

Both Jeffery and his escort say almost together, "What?"

"Mr. Portman, we were making the wire transfer of your funds to your Swiss account as you directed. My people hit the send command. Your account here was debited, but there is no received response. They followed up the best they could. The transfer appears to have disappeared."

***

Jeffery left Panama close to four that afternoon. As soon as they were off the ground, his escort was on the phone. Jeffery can't hear him but it's not good. He keeps looking at Jeffery shaking his head.

They touch down at Teterboro just after nine. There's a limo waiting with two of Jeffery's escort's brethren. Jeffery is invited to get into the car. The mob's northeast office is in Newark, in a large warehouse. Jeffery has been here twice before, never under pleasant circumstances. The limo drives into the warehouse, and Jeffery is taken to a plush office in the back. Big Bruno is holding court.

"Jeffery," he starts, "I understand WE have a problem. Where did my money go?"

A flippant reply, "Ask my escort. He was with me the entire trip. He had my laptop. Do you think I magically willed your money into the ether? We gave the money to Juan, the bank manager. He counted it in front of us and gave me this receipt. He then gave the briefcase to his teller and directed her to transfer it to your Swiss account. Either the Banco la Hacienda or the Zurich branch of the Gringotts Bank took the money."

After a few minutes of thought, Bruno tells his minions to give Jeffery his laptop and directs him to see if he can trace the money transfer. He pulls up the mob's account at la Hacienda. They see that a million was deposited earlier that day, and fifteen minutes later, it was transferred to … and this is where the trail goes blank. Next, Jeffery opens the mob's account at the Gringotts Bank. There is over seventy million in US dollars but no record of a deposit today. "Mr. Bruno, I can find no record of a transfer today, only the initial deposit. I suggest a discussion with Juan is called for."

Jeffery is allowed to leave later that night. Big Bruno dispatches his limo to take Jeffery home. He is not happy and probably will get little sleep. Jeffery speculates Juan in Panama is in for an unpleasant day tomorrow.

17 Debriefing

The limo drops Jeffery off in front of his brownstone. Lights are on, but Wanda and the kids are not there. "Great," he's thinking, "Dillion and his people are waiting for me."

It's a regular reception committee. Me, Dillion, Sydney, and a new face. A young lady in her early thirties.

Dillion starts, "Jeffery, you know almost everyone. This is Dr. Susan Kenrick; she's our financial forensic expert. You met her earlier. We brought her on board to work with Sydney."

Sydney tells me they successfully intercepted the wire transfer earlier today. It was redirected to an FBI account in the Bahamas. He believes their efforts were fully concealed."

With a grin on his face, Jeffery tells them of the near heart attack Juan had then he follows up by describing his meeting with Big Bruno. "I accessed both accounts, and there was no record of a transfer other than the initial transfer attempt by the Banco la Hacienda, and one million dollars disappeared from the mob's account. I've never seen Bruno so pissed. I'm here, so they see my hands as being clean ... for now."

"How did you do it so clean and seamless?" Jeffery asks Sydney.

"We knew your approximate arrival time, and with Dr. Kenrick's help, we kept a continuous live monitor on the bank's electronic activities. The only wire transfer occurred shortly after two today, so assuming it was yours, we hijacked it."

As they were talking, I came over to Jeffery and asked for his belt and shirt. Jeffery was wired with the same gizmos I wore when taking down Big Bear. The battery was good for up to twelve hours. The charge lasted long enough to catch all the day's events on video. Dillion is ecstatic. His case against Big Bruno is growing.

"Okay, what's next," asks Jeffery.

Dr. Kenrick speaks up, "Please, it's Susan; doctor is too formal. What I suggest is we let you process a few more deposits. I'd like to get a little more detail. When and how funds are deposited into the feeder accounts. Who tells you new funds are there that need to be moved? I've looked into these accounts; each has a few thousand dollars and appears inactive other than for the deposit and transfer of funds every few weeks. And perhaps we can identify the source of the funds. Jeffery, can you get me tapped into the bank's video system? I want to see who is making these deposits."

"When can I get the passwords for the mob's numbered accounts," asks Sydney.

"I prefer to keep a close hold on them until we are ready to drain the accounts," responds Jeffery. "There is a record each time an account is accessed. I need to be able to account to Bruno's people for each log-on; his people closely monitor the accounts. I conduct a periodic review to ensure everything is as it should be and report my findings to Bruno. One of Big Bruno's checks and balances. He has a very low level of trust."

"Besides, I want the honor of pulling the plug," Jeffery says.

***

Two months go by. There are several cash deposits in the feeder accounts, each giving Susan a face to work with. The FBI can attach names to several. Most work at nightclubs or other businesses controlled by the mob. Dillion ups his surveillance. He requests the Treasury Department's help in tracking cash flow. Using bank deposit records, cash flow information, and old IRS filings, it becomes apparent there are significant discrepancies between sales and reported income for all these businesses. Magically illicit bank deposits match these discrepancies.

I moved in with Jeffery, if for no other reason than to provide Jeffery some level of security in addition to his FBI minders.

Jeffery calls Wanda a couple times a week. A typical call:

> *"Wanda, it's me; how are you and the kids doing? I miss you; the house is too quiet."*
>
> *"I'm ready to come home. I take it your problems aren't solved yet. Please do what needs to be done so we can be together as a family."*
>
> *I'm working on it. Your father is helping. He's brought together a team that is crafting the solution. I think we can bring it to closure in a month or six weeks."*
>
> *"My god, another month? We're growing roots here. I've enrolled the twins in the local school, they are making new friends. I've even been asked to join the PTA."*

And the call continues with the expected talking points; I miss you, I miss the kids, I want to be home, why is this happening to us, etc.

After one such call Jeffery and I are talking.

"Life was so much simpler before I called asking for help," Jeffery says.

68

"As I recall, your choice was to be blackmailed into making sketchy money transactions which would have resulted in criminal charges or being killed by the mob when they found you appeared to be diddling their hidden accounts. Not great choices. And to top it off, putting your family's safety at risk. Hang in there Jeffery; the end is in sight."

"Do you think your boss has any idea this is happening?" I ask.

"He knows something is up, Bruno told him of the lost transfer in Panama. Last week he called me into his office asking how I thought this could have happened. I played dumb, telling him I knew how to make shadowy wire transfers but did not know how to hack into a banking system. As an afterthought, I was thinking I could have fed him Sydney," he said wistfully.

"Changing the topic," I say. "Wanda and the twins are doing as well as expected. My security network has detected no breaches. As for her friends, they still think she is in Florida. I've arranged for touristy postcards to be sent to them every few weeks, as well as making updates on her social media showing her and the twins on the beach or at other local attractions. Eyeball's 'propaganda' experts are creative."

"And talking about Wanda," says Jeffery, "I have a favor to ask. If anything happens to me, give this to Wanda. It will give her access to my Swiss account. It's legitimate; I've reported it annually on my tax returns. This ledger accounts for all deposits, each from a lawful source. Wanda is listed as a co-owner. For the time being, you keep the ledger."

18 Day of Reconning

In late fall, Dillion calls us together. "I think it's time we strike. Susan has documented a credible list of players." I've been working with federal prosecutors; they are chomping at the bit to file charges. My friend, Judge Hopewell on the Manhattan Third District Court, has provided me several arrest and search warrants.

"Jeffery, are you and Sydney ready to do your thing? I want the mob's account drained tonight at midnight. Can you hit them all at once?"

"Yes" answers Jeffery, "Susan helped craft a program that attacks all their accounts simultaneously. We push the button at midnight, and the accounts will be empty by 12:05 a.m."

Looking around the room, he points to six or seven agents lining the back wall. "My team will execute the warrants at midnight tonight. "Jack, did you coordinate with the NYPD?"

"Yes," said one of the agents, obviously a man of few words.

"Okay team, let's get on with it," Dillion says with some enthusiasm.

Later that night I'm sitting in the conference room with Jeffery, Sydney, and Susan. They each are manning a computer. I have a police scanner monitoring the airwaves.

"Okay Jeffery, are you ready to irrevocably change your life?" I ask. "Once we start, you're their target. Wanda and the twins are safe. No one is looking for them."

We're all watching the clock on the wall. As the secondhand approached midnight, Jeffery's finger hovers over his keyboard. He punches the enter key just as the secondhand hits its zenith.

"This account is draining faster than a bathtub on Saturday night," notes Susan.

Sydney is laughing, "This one is emptying faster than a shot of whiskey in the hand of a drunk."

By 12:04, the mob's stockpile of ill-gotten gains is safely residing in a Bahamian bank. The few minute's activities resulted in $837 million being deposited in the FBI's account.

The police scanner springs to life. Coordinated raids are being conducted in three of New Your City's boroughs and northern New Jersey.

By five that morning, seven business establishments have been shut down, and fifteen mob members were in custody.

Big Bruno was the first to fall, followed quickly by his lieutenants.

Jack had the honor of bringing Bruno in. He later reported that when his team entered through the splintered front door, they found Bruno cowering in a closet. He was perp-walked to the paddy wagon ... in his PJs.

By noon the following day, most of the targeted mob members had been arrested, most but not all.

In the following days, police brought in mob runners, those Susan identified as making deposits. A half dozen more establishments were closed.

A couple weeks later, Sydney, Jeffery, and I were leaving the federal prosecutor's office after Sydney and Jeffery provided their depositions. We were headed to a restaurant on the next block. A white sedan pulled alongside us and started firing. I hit the pavement pulling Sydney, who was next to me, down. The car squealed around the corner and was gone. Jeffery was down, blood flowing from his chest. I attempted to stanch the flow but it was ineffective; a bullet had hit one of his main arteries. His last words were, "Take care of my family," and he was gone.

19 Wanda

My first thought was how to tell Wanda. I knew they had some rough times, but she loved Jeffery. She was royally pissed when she found out about Jeffery's mob connections. She was not happy about having to go into hiding. But she loved him.

I called Anderson, told him what happened, and asked if I could use the Gulfstream. "It will be at Teterboro by three today. What else can I do?"

"I don't know, probably nothing. I have to talk to Wanda. Yes, there is one thing, call Mark and have him meet me at the airstrip." I respond.

By then, Dillion and some federal marshals emerge from the Federal Courthouse. Sirens are blaring, and police cruisers have closed down the street. The first officer on the scene asks what I saw. "A late model white sedan. It turned south at the corner. I didn't see the plate."

He relays that information to the dispatcher, who puts out an urgent notice to all police vehicles. A few minutes later the car is found abandoned.

I'm standing with Dillion; his first words are, "Shit, we didn't get them all."

"Dillion, I'm flying to Lakeview at three today to break the news to Wanda. Will you take care of things here?"

I'm landing at the Lakeview airstrip by eight, East Coast time, five pacific time. Mark is parked by the hangar in a Lakeview Police Ford LTD. I get in, he hits the flashing lights, and we're headed across town to the safe house. I ask him to kill the lights before we get there.

Wanda was distraught at getting the news but not surprised. Apparently, she and Jeffery had several recent discussions, and he shared his remorse about going down this path.

The next day we all returned to New York. On the plane, I was mostly quiet, following Wanda's lead. She explained to the children their daddy was gone, and they were going home to honor him. Arnold asked me what happened. "I'll tell you later Arnold. Now is not a good time; your mother is very sad and needs you by her side."

At one point Wanda says, "Dad, I'm thinking of staying in Lakeview; life is so much simpler. The kids have made some good friends, and I'm happy there."

"Wanda, I'll support you in whatever you want to do. Before you make any final decisions, let the current turmoil settle."

Dillion has his people meet us at the airport and takes us to the Portman brownstone. Wanda is somewhat reluctant but finally agrees to stay there.

Dillion has arranged for an FBI agent to stay with Wand, Sarah Wilson. She is in her mid-40s, physically fit and understanding, and she won't let Wanda and the kids out of her sight.

Three days later, Jeffery is buried. Dillion suggests we return to the safehouse in Oregon until Big Bruno's hit men are caught. He's heard nothing of threats against Jeffery's family, but he'd rather not risk their safety. Wanda agrees but asks for an extra day in the city.

I spend the evening with Wanda as she starts to close up the house. Actually, there is very little she wants to take. She decides the furniture will go with the house, and the accumulated clutter of knickknacks, kitchenware, dinnerware, etc., will be donated to Goodwill.

The kids have been put to bed for the last time in the brownstone. Wanda is exhausted after the funeral and a final walkthrough of the hose. She heads to bed, leaving Sarah and me in Jeffery's study.

"Would you care for a drink?" I ask Sarah. "Jeffery has some fine Glenfiddich Scotch here."

"I'm tempted, but no, not while I'm on duty. Perhaps I can join you some other time. Can I ask you a question?"

"Yes, as long as it's not about me."

"Now that's not fair," she responds. "Dillion has high praises for you. But I question his objectivity, you both being alpha males. Tell me about Lakeview. What's the story?"

I spend the next forty-five minutes telling her my tale of the North Korean spies, being an FBI fugitive, a doctor, and a deputy sheriff, all in the span of one year.

"Surely you're exaggerating," she says. "And you haven't even mentioned taking down a cartel boss or your adventures in Iraq that Dillion mentioned."

"I'll save those stories for another time. What about you?"

Sarah gives me an overview of her background. Born as Sarah Riddell, she grew up in Kansas, parents still living, two siblings, both married and still living in their hometown. She went to the University of Kansas on a sports scholarship. She graduated with BS and MS degrees in Industrial Engineering. Fifteen years ago, on a dare, she applied to the FBI; and was accepted. She met her future husband, David Wilson, at the FBI academy. They were married for eleven years and had one son, who is now in college. Her husband was diagnosed with inoperable cancer. She has been a widow for the past three years.

On that sad note, I offer my condolences and suggest we get some sleep. I'm staying in the guest room upstairs. Sarah has made a nest for herself in Jeffery's office, which gives her good tactical control of the downstairs area.

The next morning Wanda and I visit an upscale realtor to put her house on the market. Becky, a perky real estate agent, I'm guessing she just got her relator's license, thinks $1.6 million is a fair price.

"$1.6," I say, "similar homes on this street recently sold for over two million. Wanda, I think we should talk with another realtor."

As I'm getting up, a senior realtor who has been listening in pipes up, saying, "I'm sorry, we thought you wanted a quick sale."

"I do," says Wanda, "a quick sale, but not at a giveaway price."

I suggest the house be listed at $1,950,000.

20 Home

The following day Dillion whisks us to the waiting FBI Gulfstream at Teterboro Airport. As we're taking off Arnold asks, "What are these iron rings for? They're bolted to the floor."

"They are safety features," I say, "sometimes the FBI has to fly people to other places, and the rings are used to help keep them in their seats."

Millie joins the conversation. "Grandpa, can you demonstrate on Arnold how they are used?"

Wanda laughs at this, her first smile since the news of Jeffery's death. She continues, "Kids, how would you like to live in Lakeview permanently?"

"You mean not go back to our home in the city?" responds Millie.

"Yes, I mean we stay in Lakeview. You've made friends there. I think more friends than you have in New York. You like the school. And there is always Jake's where you can borrow a horse. And don't forget Flo's, Saturday's breakfasts are the best."

The kids look at each other, and Millie asks, "Is that what you want to do mother?"

After a moment's reflection, she says, "Yes." Looking at me, she continues, "Dad can you make this happen?"

I place a quick call on my cell. "It's a go. We will be in your office by four this afternoon," I say to the person on the other end of the call.

Scott meets us at the airfield as requested. We load the van with suitcases and head to town where I direct him to city hall. The four of us get out, and I lead them into the building, up to the Mayor's office. Mayor Eldridge is waiting for us, along with the city's attorney.

After pleasantries, the Mayor starts, "Sean, just to be clear, you know we have leased the Hasgrow house with the FBI. The lease has a clause that allows either party to terminate the lease with a 30-day notice. I've talked with Agent Dillion and the Bureau's facility people. They would not be opposed to terminating the lease as you propose."

I turn to Wanda, "Do you want to buy the safe house?"

Surprised and shocked she says, "Yes."

Arnold and Millie are saying, "Yes, yes, yes please."

"Okay, let's get on with it," I say to the Mayor.

The city's attorney opens his briefcase and pulls out some documents. "Mr. Murphy, who is the purchaser, you or your daughter?"

"My daughter. The title should be in Wanda Portman's name."

"The agreed sale price is $2.5 million. I understand this is a cash transaction, so I need one-third down and the balance at closing," the attorney says.

"This is a first for me," I say as I pull out my checkbook and write a check for one million dollars.

Wanda's flabbergasted, "You can't do that Dad!"

"That money is from the bounty I earned last year capturing Sa'd Ibn Atiq. You can pay me back when you sell your house."

We leave city hall with Wanda in a daze and the kids bubbling over. Back in the van, I told Scott that we had just bought the house and closing would be in a month.

"I guess that means Wanda will be evicting Nellie and me?" Scott observes with a chuckle.

"No, no," Wanda says, "you and Nellie can stay as long as you like. You're almost part of the family now."

"Dillion told me this might happen. Nellie and I submitted our retirement papers yesterday. We plan to move to New Mexico at the end of the month. She has two younger sisters there. This is a retirement long in the planning. You just helped nudge it along."

Wanda turns on me, "What did you tell Dillion?"

"I suggested to him a couple days ago that you may want to stay in Lakeview. He wishes you and the kids the best. There are far worse places to live, he said."

Later that evening, I pulled out Jeffery's ledger. "Wanda, Jeffery has an account in Switzerland for a small business he ran on the side. He started it shortly after going to work for Jeb Wilson at the investment firm. It has a bit over $17 Million in it. It is legitimate! I had Dillion's people check it out. This ledger documents all transactions. Jeffery has been declaring it for years on his tax returns. You are named as a joint owner."

The following day before Wanda is out of bed, Becky calls, excitement visible in her voice. "Mr. Murphy, is Wanda there? We have a bidding war for the house. The latest bid last night was for $2.3 million. I need to know what Wanda wants to do. Do we accept it or hope for more?"

Sit tight; we will call you back in an hour.

It's ninety minutes later by the time Wanda is up and has a cup of coffee in hand.

She calls Becky. "I understand there is some interest in my house."

I can visualize Becky, probably too excited to sit. "The latest bid price is up to $2.4!"

"I can live with that," says Wanda. "Accept it. We need to figure out how to do a long-distance closing. I don't plan on being in New York anytime in the near future."

***

At Dillion's direction, the FBI's plane is waiting for me. I invite the plane's crew to Flo's for an early breakfast. Mark is also there. Rossie greets us with her normal good humor. "I see Deputy Mark, and our former acting sheriff is bringing me some new customers. What can we get you? And Sean, you no longer get the lawman's discount."

I turn to Rossie, "How about a seniors discount?"

Mark pulls me aside and asks for my advice. "Amanda wants me to become a full-time deputy, leave Eyeball and work for her."

"What do you want to do? Speaking for Anderson, I know you have his full support."

"Making it a bit more sticky, Rebecca and I, Rebecca is one of the deputies, have something going. I think it might be serious."

I call Anderson and tell him of Mark's pending defection, an affair of the heart I tell him. He's looking to become a full-time lawman."

Anderson asks me to put Mark on. "Following Sean's footsteps, I see. Mark, you do what you think is best for you. You are always welcome at Eyeball, don't forget that. And one more thing, put my phone number in your Rolodex; you never know when it might be needed or when I might need you."

21 Just Another Day

Three months later Dillion and I are just leaving the Hoover Building. We were there to argue for Sydney. Dillion was proposing Sydney be given limited immunity so he could continue working with Dr. Kenrick. With his street smarts and Susan's technical skills, significant advances were being made against corporate fraud. The proposal was that if Sydney could keep his nose clean for three years and continue in his support role, all money laundering charges against him would be dropped. The FBI director was inclined to accept the proposal. Little did he know Susan had Sydney firmly in hand; he was smitten with her.

We also talked about Jeb Wilson. The FBI director wants a close review of his activities. "How he is involved with managing CIA and other restricted accounts," was one of his questions.

As we walked down E Street toward Union Station, Dillion was asking about Wanda. "Does she miss New Your City and city life?"

"No, she and the twins are as happy as a clam in its shell. Arnold is on the SYA basketball team, and Millie is into figure skating. And Wanda is finally putting her degree in finance to use. She opened a small financial adviser's business. Most folks in

Lakeview don't know of Jeffery, and if they do, perhaps they are hoping she can work some of his magic."

He veers off into my personal life. "Sarah tells me you two have been seeing a lot of each other in the past couple of months. Not that it is any of my business, but she has been my protégé for the past decade. You know she lost her husband a few years ago. I think down deep; she is still grieving for him. Don't hurt her."

"Dillion, she is a lovely woman with deep emotions. Many years ago, I lost my wife. I still miss her. I understand Sarah's loss. If I hurt her, shoot me."

As we cross the street, someone yells, "Sean!"

As I turn, Gonzales fires a couple rounds at me before Dillion can return fire. Gonzales is down in a growing pool of blood.

Dillon turns to me. I've been hit in the shoulder. He places pressure on the wound and calls 911. He tells me to hold my hand on it and sprints to the far side of the intersection where an elderly lady is down. She has a superficial wound in the leg.

The street is soon flooded with DC police cruisers and rescue vehicles. Gonzales is trying to crawl away. Dillion handcuffs him to a newspaper vending machine.

In the ambulance, we are headed to the George Washington Hospital, just a few blocks away; Dillion is asking me, "Who the hell is that?"

"That is El Honcho's nephew. Remember the cartel kingpin we bagged a few years ago? Gonzales was at Coeur d'Alene but slipped through our fingers. I thought he had enough sense to stay in Mexico. Apparently, he still bears a grudge."

83

Dillion leans back against the wall and sighs, "Just another day in the life of Sean Murphy."

End

Also by Don Allen

Check for Junk

Our hero, George Basdakis, is a likable young man who was born on the Gulf Coast to Greek parents but with a defective moral compass. Throughout the novel, he finds himself skirting the law, sometimes slipping over the legal edge. Capping his time as a Navy Lieutenant, private investigator, and smuggler of cars and people, he finds himself in self-imposed exile on Corfu, smuggling antique Greek artifacts when he and his cousin are drawn into a confrontation with Turkish authorities.

Dog Walker

Another fast-paced 'dime novel' that can be read in one afternoon on the beach or sitting in an airline coach's center seat. Our hero, Samuel Goodwin, and his dog Maxie, recently retired from the Boston Police Department's Canine Division, become entangled in Islamic terrorist plots. Sam's neighbor, a Yazidi refugee, is targeted by the former manager of the Mosel Rape Hotel, whom she recently recognized in downtown Boston. Two recently retired BPD detectives nicknamed Salt 'n Pepper, go into the PI business. Their first case, locating missing waitstaff from Boston's Chinatown restaurants, leads them to The Islamic Society of Boston. The Islamic Society has concocted a plan to poison New York City's water supply. Two ISIS terrorists sneak across the southern border, with cartel help, to become the Society's foot soldiers. The above cast of characters comes together to create a fascinating story.

www.ingramcontent.com/pod-product-compliance
Lightning Source LLC
Chambersburg PA
CBHW060058150626
46556CB00017BA/1943